DREAMWORKS & AARDMAN

Flushed Away™

The Essential Guide

Written by Steve Bynghall

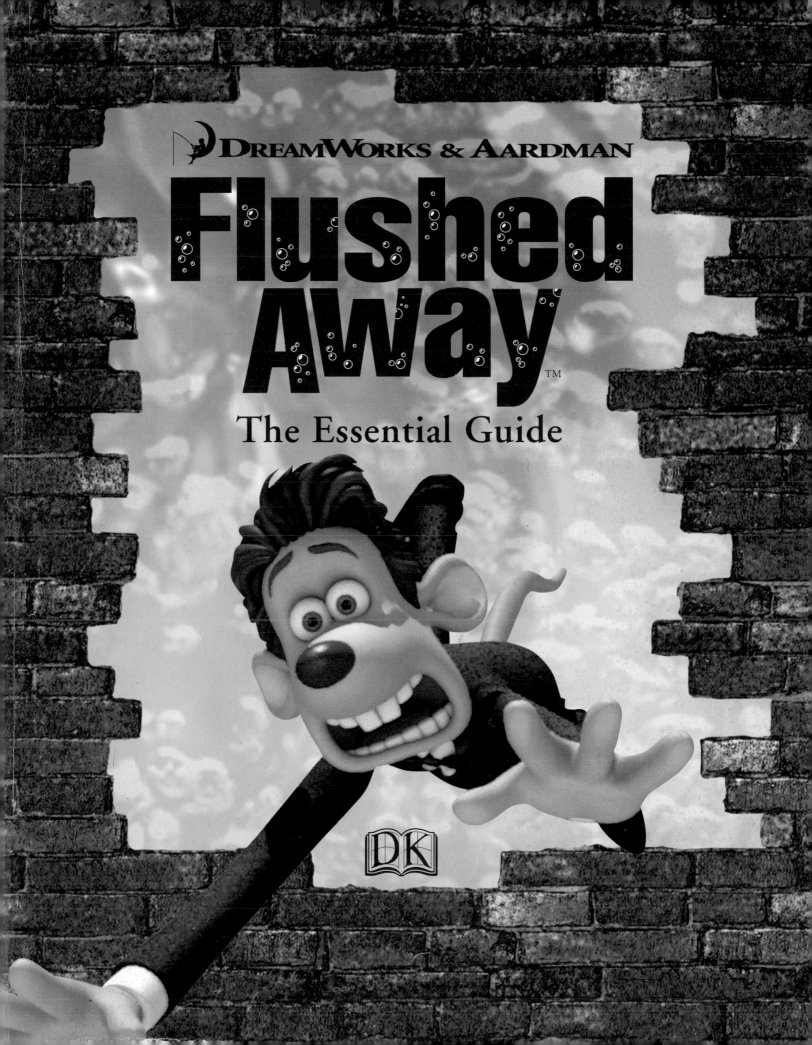

DreamWorks & Aardman

Flushed Away™

The Essential Guide

Contents

Introduction

Deep, deep underground, beneath the streets of London, England, there lurks a mysterious world. At first glance it looks very similar to the world "up top," but it is inhabited by rats, toads, frogs, slugs, fish, and a whole host of weird and wonderful creatures. And if you come and take a closer look, you will also notice that "down below" everything is made of recycled material.

However, this subterranean world is secretly under threat from a sinister plot, and suddenly it's up to one posh rat to save the day. The only problem is, he's never done anything heroic before in his life! But all that is about to change for Roderick St. James of Kensington.

Pampered Pet

Roderick St. James of Kensington is one of the most pampered pets in London. This refined rodent has always lived a life of luxury. Suave, sophisticated, and charming, he likes the finer things in life and is keen to show everyone (including himself) that he has it all.

Golden cage

In reality, Roddy is a family pet who lives in a luxury cage. Although lovingly cared for by his owner, Tabitha, he is lonely and his only "friends" are dolls.

Anyone for polo?

Roddy leads a life of leisure and, being an aristocratic rat, enjoys typically posh pursuits such as a polo. Although when Roddy plays, he rides a toy horse and has no opponents, which means he always wins!

The lap of luxury

With its fabulous furnishings and tasteful decorations, Roddy's apartment is a palace for a pampered pet. The spacious corridors of the Kensington residence provide a safe and sumptuous setting for Roddy to spend his days lounging around. With each room furnished for comfort and complete with all the latest gadgets, Roddy hardly ever sets foot outside— he just doesn't see the need to.

The kitchen has all the most expensive appliances, but Roddy's owners prefer to eat out at London's finest restaurants.

The long hall, adjoining the spacious living room, is a great place for Roddy to ride in his toy car.

Roddy is London's most eligible bachelor rat, or so he would like to believe. He always dresses to impress—from his white, monogrammed robe, to his made-to-measure tuxedo.

Roddy's personalized robe is made of the softest cotton.

Roddy keeps a supply of candy, in case he ever has visitors.

RoDDy FActS

★ Roddy lives in Kensington, one of the most exclusive areas in London.

★ He has refined tastes and prefers a cheese fondue to a cheese sandwich.

★ Roddy loves to go on skiing vacations and he's a big fan of James Bond.

Sid

Loud and brash, Sid is a common sewer rat through and through. He is an opportunistic long-tailed lout who will be your best buddy as long there's something in it for him. Sid loves to eat, and then eat some more. Maybe that's why he lets out such enormous belches!

"GOoOOAaallLL!"

Football crazy

Soccer-mad Sid loves watching football and his favorite team is Ratchester United, with their star player Wayne Ratty. In a few days time, England will be playing Germany in the final of the World Cup—the most important match in years. Thanks to his recent change of scene, not only will Sid be cheering England on with the rest of the country, but he will be watching it on Roddy's enormous stage-of-the-art widescreen TV!

Rat mates

Sid can't believe his luck when he ends up in Roddy's luxury home. In fact he loves it there so much that he invites himself to stay! Sid believes that Roddy would make an excellent butler, but is Kensington big enough for the both of them?

"Lovely jubbly"

Hair, in desperate need of a wash

Dirty rat

What lives in a sewer, smells like a sewer, and has a mouth like a sewer? Sid, of course! With his enormous belly, filthy clothes, and bad breath, Sid has some serious personal hygiene issues. Just don't get too close...

Big mouth, perfect for eating constantly

Grubby vest, made out of an old pair of underpants

Sid's pride and joy—his battered old leather jacket

Roddy tries to convince Sid that the toilet is a deluxe Jacuzzi so that he can use it to flush him back to the sewers. Sid doesn't fall for it—he may be dirty, but he isn't stupid!

A sewer rat's favorite type of pants—drainpipe jeans!

Sneakers with extra ventilation to let out the moldy cheese smell.

Flushed Away

Roddy's plan to rid himself of Sid completely backfires. Roddy falls hook, line, and sinker for the cunning sewer rat's double bluff, and it is he who ends up being flushed down the toilet instead of Sid. As a result, Roddy is about to find out what lurks beneath the streets of London.

"Whoo...ooaaah!"

Helping hand

Sid is a friendly fellow, but he gives Roddy much more than a pat on the back! After a sharp push from Sid, Roddy teeters on the edge of the toilet rim until he finally loses his balance and topples in.

Although Roddy likes exciting sports like skiing, he hadn't planned on adding diving to his list of hobbies!

"Bon Voyage, Roddy!" Sid uses all his body weight to turn the toilet lever.

LonDoN fAct

Did you know that every Londoner uses an average of 165 liters (43½ gallons) of water per day? Most of this is used for showering, laundry, drinking, and of course flushing the toilet!

Sid uses his cheap watch to distract Roddy.

Home alone

With Roddy gone, Sid has the house to himself and can start having fun. His new surroundings are a contrast to the dark, damp sewers, and he can't decide where to go first. The kitchen packed full of exquisite nibbles or the comfortable couch and widescreen TV? Sid is spoilt for choice!

Whirlpool

Once Roddy is in the water he pleads with Sid not to the pull the lever, but Sid shows no mercy. As the water rushes round and round like a menacing whirlpool, Roddy gets sucked down into the toilet's current. The posh pet starts to panic—he can't even swim!

In the Pipes

After being flushed away, Roddy finds himself twisting and turning through a massive maze of greasy drainpipes and grimy tunnels. As he slides down faster and faster, Roddy's panic turns to terror. Finally he plunges into a dark and wet sewer, with a plop.

Finding Roddy: In the sewer Roddy catches a goldfish who's looking for his dad.

Go with the flow

What's brown, lumpy, and floats down the sewer? The half-wrapped chocolate bar which Roddy clings on to in a desperate attempt to stay afloat, of course!

"Aaarr...gggh!"

Slug city

The sewers are home to millions of slugs. The slimy drain-dwellers get a shock when they see Roddy. A chorus of screams echoes round the sewers—both from the slugs and from Roddy!

I want to go home

Roddy feels drained and dishevelled. He's wet, cold, and scared, and his luxury home seems a world away. The dripping sewer walls and dark tunnels make Roddy feel even more homesick, and he wishes that this was all just a bad dream.

Light at the end of the tunnel

After stumbling around in the darkness, Roddy thinks he has found an escape route when he sees light streaming from behind a metal hatch at the end of a tunnel. The rumble of noise gives Roddy hope that help is not far away. As he bravely swings open the hatch, he lands head first in the middle of an underground Piccadilly Circus.

Poor, scared Roddy's filthy and wet clothes cling to his fur, as he wrings out his tail.

Down Below

Beneath the streets of London lurks a bustling underground city full of historical buildings, amazing shops, and colorful characters. It looks very similar to the world above, but down below everything is made out of recycled materials.

An outdoor ice rink for rodent recreation

A good old London sewer bus

"Big Ben" is made from a washing machine, a picture frame, and an old clock.

One of London's famous black boot

From busy rats scurrying about their daily busines, to street performers entertaining the crowds, eccentric old ladies walking their pet cockroaches, and prophets predicting the end of the world, life is never dull!

LoNDoN FaCT

London is the 9th largest city in the world, but did you know that the traffic is so busy in Central London that it moves at an average of 10 miles per hour—the same speed as it did in 1911?

The famous Piccadilly Circus jumbotron

Shop 'til you drop!

Rats love a bargain and there are plenty of places for some rodent retail therapy. From sewer supermarkets to places like the Bargain Bin (where you can buy all sorts of junk at great prices), shops come in all shapes and sizes. Naturally there are more cheesemongers than anything else. A special day out is a visit to the famous Drains Department Store with its ratswear department and amazing cheese hall, stopping off to have tea at the Ratz Hotel on the way home.

Getting Around

The sewer is packed full of different types of transportation and the resourceful rodents can make a vehicle from almost anything that gets flushed down the drains. Young rat pups love to collect these transportation trading cards—they're the coolest thing in the sewers this year!

Sewer citizens get from A to B using these forms of public transportation. Lots of rats pedal their way to work whilst a taxi ranks as one of the quickest ways to get around!

Taxi

This sewer taxi is made out of some cans and an old boot. This vehicle is perfect for rodents who like to travel in style and comfort.

Speed (mph)	2.5
Seats	4
Eco-rating (1-10)	4
Price (sewer pounds)	100
Wow factor (1-10)	5

Tour Bus

Made out of an oil drum, the open-top bus transports tourists around the city. It's not so good for sewers with dripping roofs!

Speed (mph)	1.5
Seats	36
Eco-rating (1-10)	7
Price (sewer pounds)	280
Wow factor (1-10)	1

Double-decker Bus

This double decker is the cheapest way to get around London. But why do you have to wait for ages and then three come at once?

Speed (mph)	2
Seats	36
Eco-rating (1-10)	7
Price (sewer pounds)	300
Wow factor (1-10)	2

Egg Whisk Bike

You just can't beat a bit of pedal power and this egg whisk bicycle is perfect for the eco friendly rat-about-town.

Speed (mph)	1.0
Seats	1
Eco-rating (1-10)	10
Price (sewer pounds)	10
Wow factor (1-10)	5

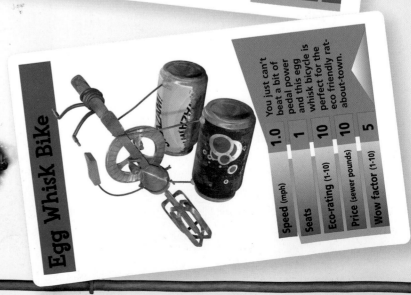

Luxury Mixer

This mixer boasts a range of added extras including an alarm and alloy whisks. It's perfect for mixing with the fashionable rats!

Speed (mph)	6
Seats	1
Eco-rating (1-10)	2
Price (sewer pounds)	400
Wow factor (1-10)	10

Racer Mixer

This sporty vehicle is compact and streamlined with extra turbo power. With its flame motif, this vehicle is stylish and speedy.

Speed (mph)	7
Seats	1
Eco-rating (1-10)	1
Price (sewer pounds)	500
Wow factor (1-10)	10

Sporty Mixer

This mean machine is sturdy and reliable. It also features a top-of-the-range padded seat to blend comfort and practicality.

Speed (mph)	5
Seats	2
Eco-rating (1-10)	3
Price (sewer pounds)	200
Wow factor (1-10)	7

These mixers are the speediest vessels in the sewers. Made out of old electric whisks, the evil hench-rats use them to chase the *Jammy Dodger*. When they go fast enough, they can do wheelies in the water!

Jammy Dodger

It might look a bit rubbish, but this is no heap of junk! The *Jammy Dodger* is reliable and much faster than it looks.

Speed (mph)	4
Seats	2
Eco-rating (1-10)	5
Price (sewer pounds)	priceless
Wow factor (1-10)	9

Rita has lovingly outfitted the *Jammy Dodger* with more gadgets and added extras than any other vehicle in the sewer. The rubber duck has the least number of gadgets.

Roadster

Rodents love to travel in style. Made out of an old battery, this open-top vehicle is a stylish way to cruise the sewers.

Speed (mph)	3.5
Seats	2
Eco-rating (1-10)	4
Price (sewer pounds)	350
Wow factor (1-10)	7

Rubber Duck

You certainly won't want to travel by rubber duck if you're in a hurry. This vehicle only goes as fast as the sewage flows!

Speed (mph)	0.2
Seats	1
Eco-rating (1-10)	10
Price (sewer pounds)	350
Wow factor (1-10)	-1

Rita

Smart, cunning, and beautiful, Rita uses her wits to survive in the murky world beneath the streets of London. Although she often uses her sharp tongue to put people in their place—especially Roddy—she is very loyal to her family and friends, and always keeps her promises.

Red hair to match her fiery temperament

Jammy Dodger

Rita is the captain (and only crew member) of her trusty ship, the *Jammy Dodger*. She skilfully navigates her way through the dangers of the sewers and is Roddy's only hope of finding his way back home. When she is at the helm of her boat, Rita rules the waves!

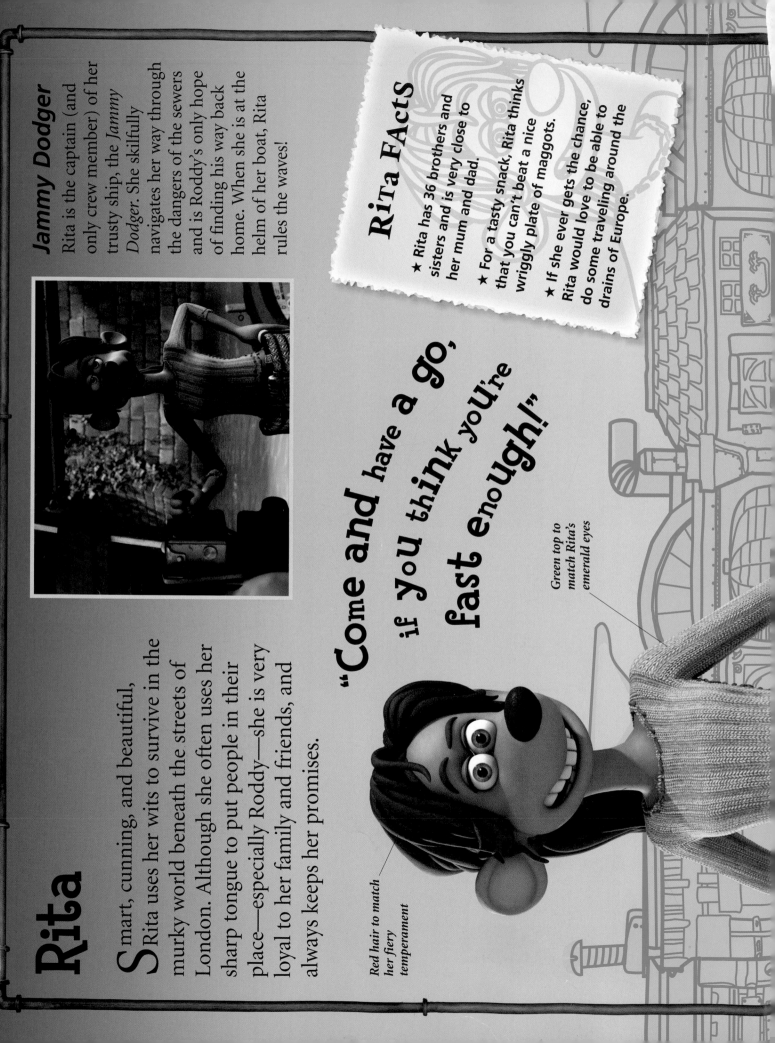

RiTa FActs

★ Rita has 36 brothers and sisters and is very close to her mum and dad.

★ For a tasty snack, Rita thinks that you can't beat a nice wriggly plate of maggots.

★ If she ever gets the chance, Rita would love to be able to do some traveling around the drains of Europe.

"Come and have a go, if you think you're fast enough!"

Green top to match Rita's emerald eyes

Rita rules!

Rita often has to defend the *Jammy Dodger*. When Roddy arrives he's about as dangerous as a moldy cheese sandwich, but the hench-rats are a different story. Fortunately Rita is a good shot with her homemade bow and arrow.

Royal ruby

Rita is desperate to recover a priceless ruby found in the sewers by her father and then stolen by The Toad. She believes it is a jewel from Queen Elizabeth's crown that fell down the drains of Buckingham Palace.

This ruby could change Rita's life forever!

Sophisticated gentleman rat, Roddy, realizes that the ruby is a fake and smashes it to prove he is right!

Rita needs a belt to hold up her pants!

Union flag pants from the city of London

Bottle-capped boots keep the sewer water out!

The Jammy Dodger

Although it looks completely unseaworthy, the *Jammy Dodger* is the fastest vessel in the pipes. Rita's beloved boat hardly ever lets her down and is rat-packed full of gadgets to help keep The Toad and his hench-rats at a safe distance.

Unique craftsmanship

Roddy calls the *Jammy Dodger* a "worthless old pile of rubbish," and in many ways this is true. The ship is made entirely out of objects recovered from the drains. However, looks can be deceiving! The vessel was ingeniously put together by Rita's father, and it has lasted for many years and saved the day many times!

Upper control panel includes the red emergency lever!

Loud horn to warn other boats to move out of the way

Swimming goggles function as a windshield.

The hatch conceals the Jammy Dodger's mechnical arm.

The main part of the boat is made from an old tin bath.

Dinner plate stops water going down the funnel.

A clarinet acts as the boat's funnel.

Go gadgets!

In times of danger there's always a handy button to press or lever to pull on the *Jammy Dodger*. When Rita pulls one lever, it releases a custard mix and turns the water into a sticky whirlpool.

"It's going to be a bumpy ride"

Old magazines and postcards line the inside of the boat.

Rubber tire helps protect the boat during collisions.

The boat's motor is an old bicycle chain.

Propeller to cut through thick sewage

Tennis ball floats for extra buoyancy on bumpy rides

Hair carefully styled for maximum sophistication

Polished white teeth used to nibbling on the finest foods

Elegantly tailored tuxedo, made to measure

Roddy

Some might say that Roddy adds sophistication to the world below, but most think he's a posh twit! The pipes are no place for a refined creature like Roddy—he cannot cope with sewer life and just gets himself into trouble. Roddy is a good-natured guy who is not used to having any enemies. He'd do anything to get home to Kensington!

RODDY FActS

★ Roddy suffers from sea-sickness during the bumpy rides along sewer canals.

★ He hates creepy crawlies, but in the sewers he meets pet cockroaches, screaming slugs, and biting bedbugs. He even eats maggots!

★ He attends his first ever wedding in the sewers.

Action hero?

Is Roddy ready to spring into action at a hint of danger? Not on your life! Rita discovers that Roddy panics at the first sign of trouble, making him more of a liability than a lifesaver in stressful situations. While Rita keeps her wits about her, Roddy is a rat who is easily rattled!

Shiny shoes, to impress the ladies

Dropping in

Roddy and Rita's relationship gets off to a shaky start. Acting on a tip-off, Roddy goes in search of the *Jammy Dodger*, hoping to get a lift all the way home to Kensington. Rita isn't too pleased when she finds a stowaway on board her beloved boat, and uses the *Jammy Dodger*'s robotic arm to trap the helpless Roddy.

Hanging on

While Rita's world has made her bold and fearless, Roddy's lifestyle has not prepared him for high pressure situations. He tries to appear brave, athletic, and resourceful, but no one is fooled!

"I'm an innocent bystander!"

Romeo rat

Roddy is an old romantic at heart and can usually turn on the charm by crooning a tune. He tries to thaw his frosty friendship with Rita when he sings *Ice cold Rita, Won't you be sweeter to me?* which at least makes her smile!

Instead of using the toy ukulele as a paddle, Roddy begs for forgiveness with a song!

The Toad

"Goodbye, vermin!"

This evil amphibian rules the London sewer system, using a lowlife gang of hench-rats to do his dirty work. The green gangster thinks he is more important than everybody else, and considers himself to be very cultured and sophisticated. In reality, the pompous piece of pondlife has terrible taste, as well as a terrible temper!

Smart suit—what all the best-dressed London crime bosses are wearing

FluSHeD fActS

★ The Toad has a weakness for flies which he captures with his long extended tongue.

★ The Toad has a shelf full of scrapbooks detailing every part of his life, but he's the only one who ever reads them!

★ One of The Toad's fondest childhood memories is of the day he spent boating with the young prince.

Toad in the hole

The Toad runs his evil empire from his dark, damp lair. Whether issuing commands from the control room, or admiring his collection of royal memorabilia, The Toad is safe in his secret hideaway. Located in the heart of the sewers, it also includes the lethal Ice Room!

This broken pot is supposed to look like the Queen.

Royal collection

The Toad cherishes the memories of the time he spent in the royal household, and has gathered what he believes is a priceless collection of royal artefacts. In fact, the rodent-hating royalist's prized possessions are tasteless junk from the pipes.

Horrible, bulging eyes

Warty green skin which feels cold and clammy to touch

Rings fit so tightly on The Toad's fingers, that he can't take them off.

Tasteless trinkets

The Toad loves to show off his wealth and power. When he learns that Roddy is from Kensington, The Toad hopes he is a rat of "quality" who will admire the royal shrine. At first, Roddy pretends to be impressed, but when he accidentally knocks some of the kitsch collection over, The Toad gets very angry!

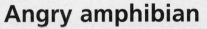

Angry amphibian

The Toad is always mean and moody, but when he gets really angry, he literally swells up with rage. When something makes him mad, such as Roddy and Rita escaping again, The Toad's throat blows up like a hideous green balloon. With idiots like Spike and Whitey messing up his plans, that means a lot of swelling!

The Toad is so mad this time, that he just might burst!

Brown shoes fit The Toad's feet snugly.

When he's in his lair thinking about getting rid of rodents, The Toad likes to wear a smoking jacket and sit in his favorite armchair.

Tragic Story

Beneath his warty exterior, The Toad hides a tragic childhood secret. When he was young he was the royal prince's favorite pet. For a time, boy and toad were inseparable, playing together at the palace every day. Until one day, the prince got a very special birthday present...

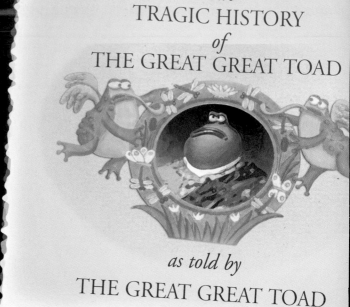

The
TRAGIC HISTORY
of
THE GREAT GREAT TOAD

as told by
THE GREAT GREAT TOAD

The Toad tells his childhood story over and over again. It might bring a lump to his throat, but it makes everybody else feel sick!

This photo shows all The Toad's friends from the royal household.

Happier times

The Toad keeps a scrapbook full of all his happy memories. This photo of him playing in the royal gardens with the young prince always brings a little tear to his eye.

For a time The Toad's childhood was idyllic, but one fateful day, everything changed. Even now, many years later, The Toad gets mad when he thinks about it!

The Toad's story takes a tragic turn on the prince's birthday. On that terrible day, the prince was given a new pet rat. Very soon the rat replaced The Toad in the prince's affections.

Le Frog has heard his English cousin's tale of woe many times.

When The Toad gets the book out, Le Frog knows he is in for a long evening!

Down the pan

Shortly after the rat arrived, The Toad found himself unwanted, until one day a servant took him to the palace toilet and flushed him away. Ever since, The Toad has hated rats and vowed to get revenge.

Spike

Macho, mean, and menacing—unfortunately Spike is none of these things. Small, wiry, and beady-eyed, Spike is the unofficial leader of the hench-rats. Although he threatens his victims with the promise of dire consequences if they don't cooperate, this not-so-vicious vermin is more useless than ruthless, and usually ends up falling flat on his face!

Accident-prone rat

Spike's clumsy antics often get him in trouble and constantly undermine his tough-rat image. In a single day Spike is catapulted into the air, tarred and feathered, and frozen in a block of ice. An innocent-looking tin of nuts causes yet another embarrassing accident for Spike.

"Alright, it's time to bring out The Persuader!"

Spiky hairstyle, the source of Spike's nickname

Small beady eyes

Nose, always ready to sniff out trouble

Shiny silver suit in super-extra small

Fists clenched, ready to thump any enemies

Spike is always encouraging Whitey to be a more confident hench-rat, even allowing him to be the first to receive a dressing down from The Toad!

Spike's tough-rat stance shows he means business.

SpIkE FActS

★ Spike's middle name is Leslie, but he doesn't like people to know because it doesn't sound very macho.

★ Spike's favorite way to frighten his victims is to bring out a nutcracker, which he calls the "Persuader"!

★ Tough-rat Spike still lives with his mom!

Rat ambitions

Spike would love to be promoted by The Toad, perhaps as hench-rat-in-charge or even as his official deputy. He is currently studying part time for a diploma in intimidation and bullying, to improve his job prospects. But, little does he know that The Toad has a sinister plan for all rodents...

Spike is always ready for a fight, and he has an impressive range of aggressive facial expressions. And if all else fails, it is time to bring out the Persuader...

Big boss

Spike is so desperate to impress the Toad that he often hides behind his partner, Whitey, and has even been known to faint in fear. He has a habit of saying the wrong thing at the wrong time—when he showed The Toad Rita's broken ruby, he comforted him by telling him it would make some nice earrings and a bracelet!

Whitey

With his broad shoulders, muscular body, and huge hands, Whitey is a fearsome sight. He lost his hair and became an albino after working as a lab rat "up top," so nowadays he is completely white, with a bald head, and a pair of piercing pink eyes. Certainly not the sharpest rat in the litter, The Toad employs Whitey for his brawn, not his brains.

Vacant expression—Whitey is often confused

Cheap, shiny suit, size XXXL

Chunky gold ring, which can also be used as a knuckle-duster

Flashy fashion

The only smart thing about Whitey is his clothes. From his sharp suits to his gold tooth, gold chain, gold buttons, gold rings, and gold buckles on his shoes, Whitey shows what all fashion-conscious hench-rats will be wearing this year.

Slip-on style shoes, because Whitey hasn't figured out how to tie shoelaces!

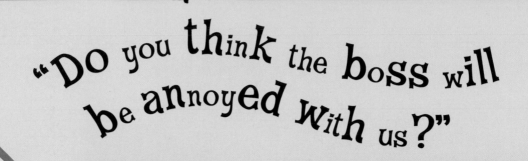

"Do you think the boss will be annoyed with us?"

WhiTey FActS

★ Whitey often hides his sensitive pink eyes behind some dark sunglasses.

★ Confused as always, Whitey thinks Roddy is called Millicent Bystander for ages.

★ Whitey likes nothing better than a spicy curry, although Spike isn't too keen to be around him afterwards!

Deadly double act

This mis-matched pair have been through thick and thin together. (Whitey is thick, Spike is thin!) Despite his size, Whitey is very insecure and he depends on his little pal for advice and leadership.

Somehow, in spite of their best efforts, this hapless duo always manage to mess things up!

Whitey is very sensitive. When his hands get cold in The Toad's Ice Room, he puts on his pink mittens, much to Spike's embarrassment!

The Hench-Rats

The Toad hires rodent heavies to do his dirty work. These long-tailed lowlifes are the dregs of the drains with few morals and even fewer brains. The bumbling bullies don't often get results and The Toad may be right when he says that they are just a bunch of "incompetent cheese eaters!"

If Spike and Whitey are his most successful hench-rats, The Toad is in serious trouble. This dim-witted duo are hopeless at following orders and seriously rubbish at scaring people. Unfortunately, the rest of the hench-rats are just as bad...

Thimblenose loves his job—he gets to flip the switch and ice poor rodents, like Roddy and Rita.

Thimblenose Ted

After having the tip of his nose sliced off in a fight, Ted wears a thimble to protect his battered nose and hide his scar. Just like his boss, The Toad, Thimblenose Ted tells a good story, and if you bump into him, the chances are you'll have to listen to the tale of how he lost the tip of his nose—again and again!

Fat Barry

The heaviest of the hench-rats, Fat Barry is the quiet one who stays in the background and actually gets things done. The rotund rodent is happy working for The Toad, as long as he gets paid in cheese.

"Arrivederci, posh bloke!"

Ladykiller wears supercool shades at all times, even indoors.

Ladykiller owns more than 50 suits but this pinstripe one is his favorite.

Ladykiller

Elegantly dressed, hair coolly slicked back, and nonchalantly chewing a matchstick, Ladykiller likes to think he has a special way with female rats. This sneaky young rat knows hundreds of chat up lines and his tiny mind often strays from the job in hand!

Frozen Out

The Toad always likes to give his enemies a frosty reception and when Roddy and Rita get on the wrong side of him, they come very close to joining his "cubist collection."

The not-so-lucky ones

The Toad describes them as "a catalogue of thieves, double-crossers, and do-gooders." They may have made the wretched rodent-hater angry for different reasons, but all the rats have been disposed of in the same ruthless way.

The Toad loves the feeling of power he has when he's at the control panel of the Ice Machine. When the levels of liquid nitrogen are high enough, he flips a switch and prepares to add Roddy and Rita to his gruesome gallery.

Cheeky Chico laughed at The Toad for his vulgar taste, but The Toad isn't very good at taking criticism!

When clumsy Roger accidentally knocked over a jar of tadpoles he knew his days were numbered. Whoops!

Ron the Rascal tried to steal Queen Victoria's bust—a cookie jar, and one of The Toad's most treasured possessions.

Roddy and Rita's relationship thaws slightly and Rita's quick thinking provides them with a means of escape.

Escape from the Ice Room

Rita uses a handy paper clip to pick the lock of the chains holding her and Roddy. The daring duo escape, leaving Spike and Whitey to get iced instead. Resourceful Rita yanks out the master electric cable from the control panel, unaware of its importance to The Toad's evil plans!

Roberta went to The Toad's lair for a fake interview and became the test subject for his cold-blooded collection!

Former hench-rat Skinny Vinnie overheard The Toad formulating his plan to get rid of all the rats in the sewer, so he got the cold shoulder.

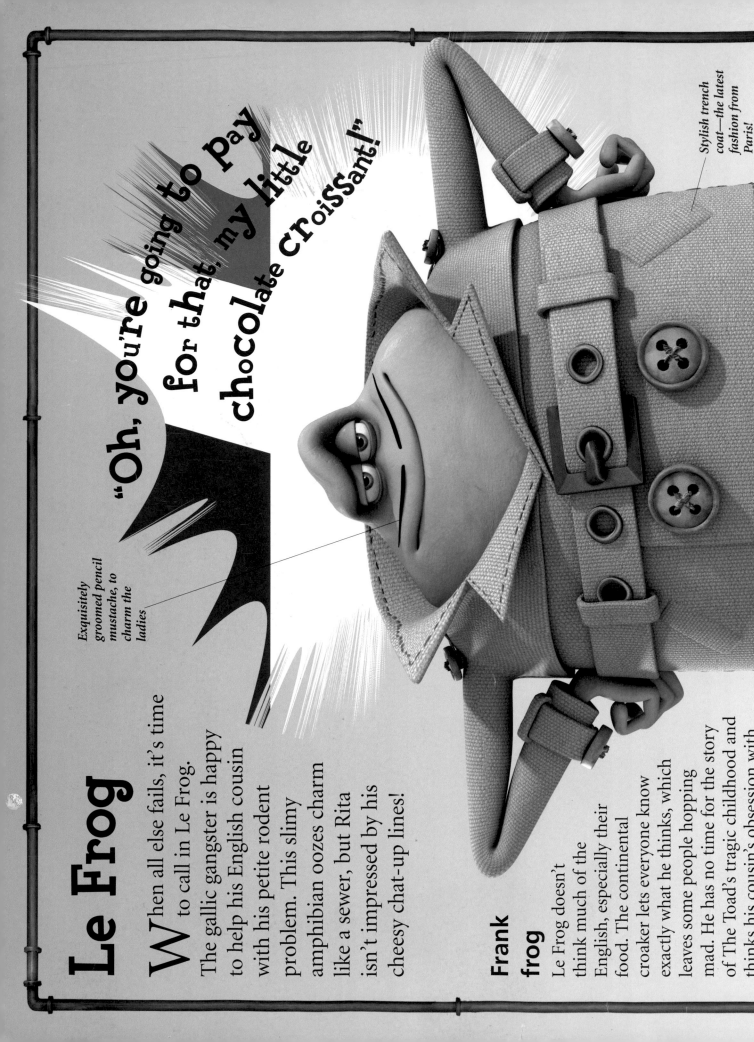

Le Frog

When all else fails, it's time to call in Le Frog. The gallic gangster is happy to help his English cousin with his petite rodent problem. This slimy amphibian oozes charm like a sewer, but Rita isn't impressed by his cheesy chat-up lines!

Exquisitely groomed pencil mustache, to charm the ladies

Stylish trench coat—the latest fashion from Paris!

"Oh, you're going to pay for that, my little chocolate croissant!"

Frank frog

Le Frog doesn't think much of the English, especially their food. The continental croaker lets everyone know exactly what he thinks, which leaves some people hopping mad. He has no time for the story of The Toad's tragic childhood and thinks his cousin's obsession with rodents is completely mad!

Le FROg FActs

★ Le Frog likes to savor his food and can spend up to five hours eating a single meal.

★ His favorite magazine is 'Allo, 'Allo, which features all the international amphibian gossip!

★ Le Frog is a proud Frenchman and loathes everything English, especially the weather, the food, and the people.

Wet suit for underwater missions

Ninja frogs

Le Frog is assisted by a loyal band of hench-frogs. These faithful French frogs dress like deadly ninjas and love to show off their impressive martial arts moves. However, the only black belts amongst this gallic group are the ones holding up their pants! In reality, they prefer eating to fighting. When Roddy spots a tasty fly, the hench-frogs get their tongues in a tangle and he is able to save Rita.

Flippers for extra speed in aquatic chases

Le Frog's ninjas are more interested in playing the accordion than getting down to business and catching Roddy and Rita.

The most outrageous hench-frog is Marcel, the mime frog. Instead of Kung Fu moves, Marcel acts out The Toad's orders using the graceful art of mime. He takes himself very seriously, but no one else does!

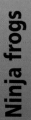

Roddy and Rita

He's a posh pet with no real friends and she's a down-to-earth sewer rat from a large family. Although Roddy and Rita don't seem to have much in common, there is definitely chemistry between them. After a shaky start, they are forced to work together, and they soon get to know each other better. Could it be a case of opposites attracting?

Rita's family

Unlike Roddy, Rita has a very close family. Being the eldest of 36 brothers and sisters means that Rita is used to looking out for everybody. When Roddy overhears Rita's cheeky little brother suggesting that they betray him to The Toad, he jumps to the wrong conclusions and accuses Rita of double-crossing him. Rita is very angry—her family would never, ever rat on anyone.

Rita has always been a very practical rat, fixing things and looking after her boat. In contrast, Roddy hasn't done a hard day's work in his entire life!

There's no "i" in team

When they are first captured by Spike and Whitey and taken to see The Toad, Roddy insists that he is innocent and denies knowing Rita. Rita thinks Roddy is a posh idiot and claims that he's an international jewel thief who has stolen the ruby. The Toad soon becomes bored of Roddy and Rita's arguing and sends them to his Ice Room to cool off.

To escape from the Ice Room, Roddy and Rita are forced to work together for the first time—although Roddy still manages to mess things up and pulls Rita's pants down!

Rita wasn't planning on showing the world her underwear, but at least it is clean!

Roddy is clinging on for dear life and hasn't even noticed Rita's predicament!

In this together

When Roddy and Rita find themselves in the clutches of Le Frog, they stick together and help each other out. This time it's Roddy's quick thinking that gets the pair out of a tight spot!

Friends at last

Over a romantic meal (of maggots!) aboard the *Jammy Dodger*, Rita admits that her first impressions of Roddy were wrong, while Roddy thanks her for saving him. They've come to realize that they stand a better chance of beating The Toad and getting Roddy home if they work as a team.

Journey Home

Rita agrees to take Roddy home to Kensington in exchange for some real jewels, but she knows that the journey will be a long and difficult one. Navigating the rapids is bad enough, but escaping the sewers is even more dangerous while being chased by The Toad and his cronies!

The Hyde Park Rapids

The most dangerous part of the voyage is the water treatment works. Not only will the waves sink the boat, but they also lead to an enormous waterfall, with a lethal drop. And, if you survive all that, you still might get boiled alive in bleach!

With a trademark Kung Fu kick, Le Frog sends the *Jammy Dodger* crashing down to the churning water below!

Don't look down!

Unfortunately, the Hyde Park Rapids prove too rough for the *Jammy Dodger* and Rita cannot stop it from going over the edge of the waterfall. Acting quickly, Roddy uses the mechanical arm to attach the boat to an overhead pipe. As it swings in mid air, Roddy and Rita cling on for dear life!

Up and away

At the last moment Roddy and Rita grab on to a plastic bag and rise rapidly, just like riding in a hot air balloon. It takes them up through a chimney right out of the sewers and into the London sky, drifting west toward Roddy's home.

London Fact

London was the first city in the world to have an underground railway network. It opened in 1863. Today about 2.5 million people use the Tube every day.

After Rita has gone, Roddy realizes what The Toad's evil plan is. He knows that he must go back to the sewers and save his friends, especially Rita. Sid must flush him away again!

Home sweet home?

Roddy and Rita eventually drop through a familiar fireplace and Roddy repays Rita with a real ruby, as promised. Before she leaves, Rita realizes that Roddy is a pet, with no family of his own, but Roddy is too ashamed to admit it.

The Evil Plan

The Toad has come up with the most dangerous, demented, and downright nasty plan to rid the sewers of rats once and for all! The top secret twisted plot involves replacing all the rodents with The Toad's tadpoles, in what he calls "a glorious amphibian dawn!"

Little does The Toad know that Roddy and Rita are about to outsmart him.

A foolproof plan

The Toad thinks his plan is perfect. At just the right time, he intends to open the main sewer floodgates. With the gates open, a huge volume of water will be released, creating a massive tidal wave. The surprised rodents won't stand a chance as the water level rises.

FLOODGATE CONTROL

FLOODGATE

The World Cup

The World Cup is the perfect time for The Toad to carry out his evil plan. England is soccer-obsessed, and everybody "up top" will be glued to their TV during the World Cup final with Germany. Of course, nobody will want to miss a second of the action, so at half time of this historic game everybody above ground will run to the toilet. As millions of people flush their toilets, it will create the rush of water The Toad needs to put his evil plan into action.

"You rodents!"

When Roddy realizes what the Toad is up to, he only has minutes left to save the day! It's time for the pampered pet to become a real hero.

Who's the daddy?

Apart from his royal collection, The Toad's tadpoles are his pride and joy. He keeps his babies safely hidden behind a curtain, and like any doting dad, he coos and fusses over them—but only when no one is looking!

DAILY RAT

POSH BLOKE SAVES CITY

BY STEVE McSQUEAK

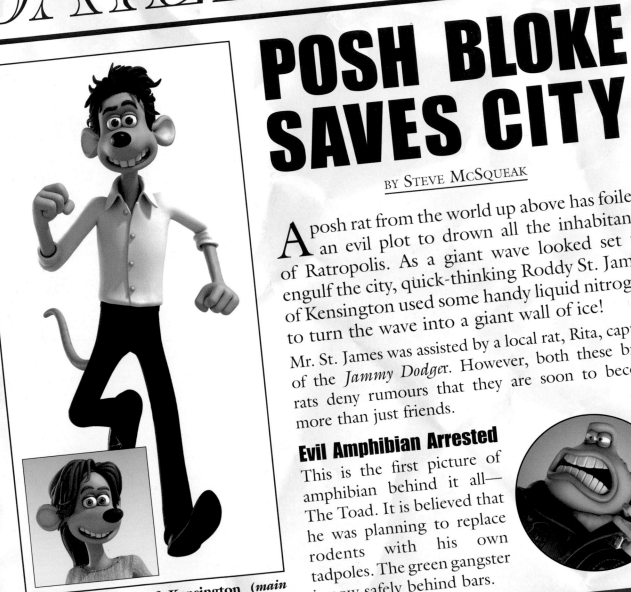

A posh rat from the world up above has foiled an evil plot to drown all the inhabitants of Ratropolis. As a giant wave looked set to engulf the city, quick-thinking Roddy St. James of Kensington used some handy liquid nitrogen to turn the wave into a giant wall of ice! Mr. St. James was assisted by a local rat, Rita, captain of the *Jammy Dodger*. However, both these brave rats deny rumours that they are soon to become more than just friends.

Evil Amphibian Arrested

This is the first picture of amphibian behind it all— The Toad. It is believed that he was planning to replace rodents with his own tadpoles. The green gangster is now safely behind bars.

Roddy St. James of Kensington (*main picture*) and the lovely Rita (*inset*.)

Full Report PLUS 4 pages of pictures inside • page 6

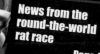
News from the round-the-world rat race

Page 63

Cooking with Gordon McRatty

Page 48

Dim Duo Duped

continued from front page

Two of The Toad's most senior hench-rats are unlikely to face charges as police can find no evidence that they knew anything about their boss's plan. Spike (right) and Whitey (left) were outraged when they discovered what The Toad was up to and are now looking for new employment.

Spike's mother also revealed that her son sustained injuries to his rear end when he landed in a jar of tadpoles during the incident.

WHO? MOI?

Le Frog, French mercenary and cousin of The Toad, was also in custody last night. It is believed that Le Frog is top of InterFrog's most wanted list and will have to go back to France to stand trial for his many crimes.

Plucky Eyewitness To Make Full Recovery

A fly, who was dramatically saved from being eaten by The Toad, is recovering in hospital. The fly is a key witness for the prosecution as he overheard The Toad talking about his plan.

Local Prophet Considers Future

A prophet, who has been preaching that a terrible flood will occur, is reported to be considering his future, since it has turned out that the end isn't nigh after all.

LONDON TO RATPOOL £25 return

RatRail

EXCLUSIVE Interview Inside SID

"THE TRUE STORY OF MY NEW LIFE UP TOP!"

DK

LONDON, NEW YORK, MUNICH,
MELBOURNE, and DELHI

Senior Designers	Guy Harvey and Anne Sharples
Senior Editor	Catherine Saunders
Publishing Manager	Simon Beecroft
Brand Manager	Robert Perry
Category Publisher	Alex Allan
DTP Designer	Hanna Ländin
Production	Rochelle Talary

First American Edition, 2006
Published in the United States by
DK Publishing
375 Hudson Street, New York, New York 10014

07 08 09 10 10 9 8 7 6 5 4 3 2

Page Design Copyright © 2006 Dorling Kindersley Limited

ISBN-13: 978-0-7566-2243-5
ISBN-10: 0-7566-2243-3

High-resolution workflow proofed by Media Development and Printing Ltd, UK
Printed and bound in the U.S.A. by Lake Book Manufacturing, Inc.

ACKNOWLEDGMENTS
Dorling Kindersley would like to thank Karen Barnash, Corinne Combs, Kristy Cox,
Rhion Magee, Liska Otojic, and Wendy Rogers at DreamWorks, Jess Houston
at Aardman, and Roger Harris for the London Pipe Link artwork .
The author would like to thank Kelly Andrews for her
contributions and support.